The Adventures of Hillary

HILLARY'S BIG BUSINESS ADVENTURE

Lori Nelson

Illustrated by Jerry Craft

THE ADVENTURES OF HILLARY
AN IMPRINT OF NELSON PUBLISHING, LLC / WASHINGTON, D.C.

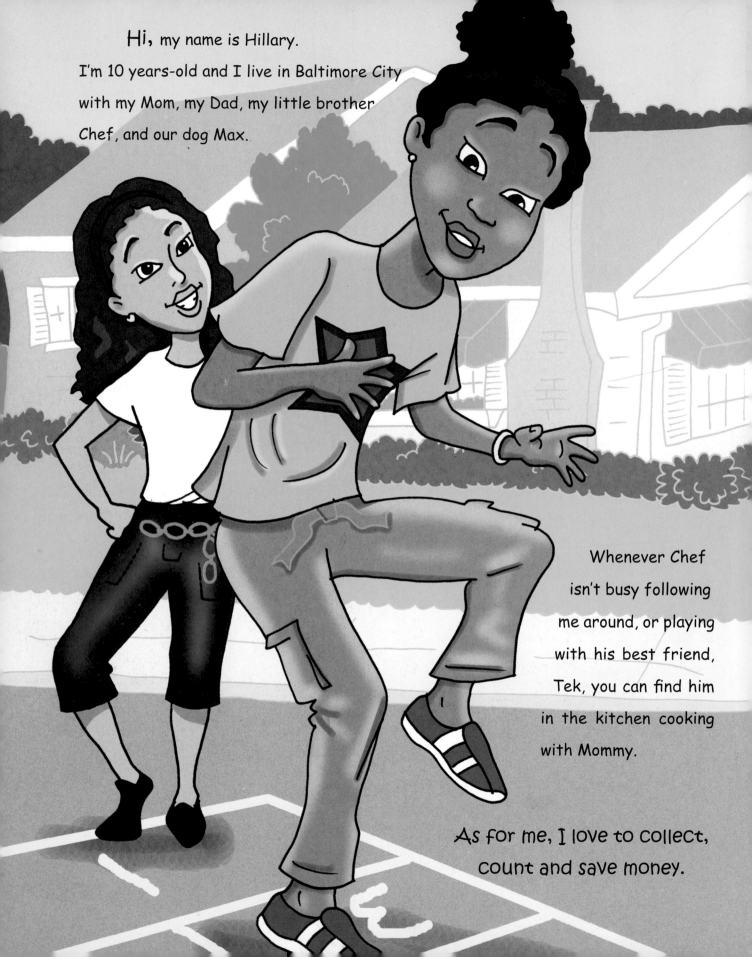

Hi, my name is Hillary.
I'm 10 years-old and I live in Baltimore City
with my Mom, my Dad, my little brother
Chef, and our dog Max.

Whenever Chef
isn't busy following
me around, or playing
with his best friend,
Tek, you can find him
in the kitchen cooking
with Mommy.

As for me, I love to collect,
count and save money.

Chef and I love to play outside during the summer with our friends.

I was outside as usual, playing hopscotch with my best friend, Zoë. Zoë is a dancer, so she moves gracefully when we play hopscotch and usually beats me. Chef was tossing his football around when Tek rode up on his brand-new electronic bike.

Tek has all the latest electronic games and toys. He takes his laptop computer everywhere he goes. I guess you could call him a computer genius.

"WOW!" we all sang together, staring in amazement. Chef and Zoë began questioning Tek about the bike, but I never said a word. I just stood there with a big smile on my face as I began to imagine myself riding the bike at the park, by the lake, chasing the birds as they flew away.

My daydream ended when I realized that Chef, Zoë and Tek were all staring at me, wondering why I was standing there so quiet with that big grin on my face.

"Hillary, are you okay?" Zoë asked.

"I'm gonna get a bike just like that!" I suddenly yelled out.

Chef and Tek began to laugh so hard that they could hardly stand up straight.

"What's so funny?" I demanded.

"Yeah, I think you could use a new bike. Like something in this century." Tek said, still bent over with laughter. "That old-fashion bike of yours should be put in a museum." he added.

"Hey, Hill's bike is a classic!" Zoë said in my defense. Tek and Chef begin to laugh even harder.

"Hillary, Tek's bike is a full suspension cruiser bike with high-tech performance stuff." Chef explained.

"So what does that mean?" Zoë asked.

"I don't know, but it sure sounds expensive. Mommy and Daddy will never pay for it." he added.

"Whatever! C'mon, Zoë, let's go make some Sweet-Potato cookies to celebrate the purchase of my new bike." I said with confidence, as I grabbed my bike from the tree it was leaning up against.

"Wait!" Chef yelled just as we turned to head for the house. "How do you plan to get Mommy and Daddy to buy you this bike, Hill?"

"Mommy and Daddy won't have to buy it. I'll buy it myself," I answered.

"And just how do you plan to pay for a bike, Hillary?" Chef asked.

"I'll tell you at the meeting," I replied.

"Meeting...what meeting?" he questioned.

"The meeting I'm planning at the clubhouse after church tomorrow. I'll reveal my business plan then," I said, then turned and walked towards my house.

"Save me some Sweet-Potato cookies!" Chef yelled. "You know they're my favorite!" he added.

After returning home from church, Chef and I ran upstairs to change out of our church clothes, then we ran to the kitchen and grabbed fruit cups, cookies and juice boxes, then headed out the door to the backyard and into the clubhouse.

The Plan

Zoë and Tek walked into the clubhouse just as Chef and I dug into our snacks. As Tek reached over and grabbed one of Chef's cookies, Zoë asked, "So what's the big business plan?"

"We're going to have a big sale!" I said with excitement.

"A what?" they asked.

"A bake sale and a garage sale all in one," I explained. "We'll call it The BIG Sale."

The Goal

"We'll all be responsible for gathering inventory for the garage sale. I'll handle the advertising and marketing for the event. Chef, since you are the cooking expert you will be in charge of organizing the baked goods. Zoë and Tek, you will be responsible for arranging the pick-up of the inventory." I ordered.

ME
ADVERTISING
CHEF
BAKED GOO
ZOE
NVENTORY
TEK

"Why should we help? What do we get out of it?" Chef asked.

"We'll split the profit four ways. I'll be able to buy my bike and we'll each be able to open up a real savings account at a real bank—instead of keeping our money in the pigs." I said, pointing to the colorful piggy banks on the back shelf. We were all excited, and after we were done discussing each person's role and the schedule, we set out to start our adventure.

The Preparation

We had two weeks to prepare for the big event. Chef arranged for all of our mothers and grandmothers to bake a variety of cakes, pies, cookies, brownies, lemon bars and fudge to be sold at the bake sale. We decided to sell the cakes and pies for $2 a slice, and the cookies, brownies, lemon bars and fudge we'd sell two for $1.

Zoë and Tek collected clothes, toys, golf clubs, dishes, knickknacks, paintings, small furniture pieces and anything else donated by our parents, grandparents, church members and even our own belongings. Daddy and Mr. Kyoko, Tek's father helped them to transport the items. We priced everything from $1 to $50, depending on its value. We even had a beautiful antique dining table donated by my grandmother that we priced at $80.

I began working on the advertising and marketing materials. I went around the house collecting poster boards, glue, glitter, stickers, magic markers, and decorative ribbon to create beautiful signs to hang around the neighborhood to tell people about the sale. I hung signs at church, the supermarket, the library, and the recreation center. I even hung signs at Zoë's dance studio and Chef and Tek's baseball field. Daddy drove me around for an hour two days in a row helping me hang up all the signs.

The BIG Event

After two weeks of planning, organizing, collecting and advertising, the big day was finally here. The beautiful, bright yellow sun was a clear sign that the weather would be perfect for the sale. We got up early Saturday morning to set up the tables, string balloons, and prepare to work our stations.

THE BIG SALE

Zoë and Tek's job was to manage the main inventory. Chef's job was to manage the baked goods station. Everything looked so delicious. We were having a hard time remembering that the sweets were for the customers, not for us to eat. I was in the middle of it all with the cash box, keeping an eye on everything. By 9 a.m., we were ready for business.

Our parents sat on the porch watching as the first customers of the day arrived. People would look around, maybe ask a few questions, and then most would leave with a purchase.

Our parents, a bit surprised, told us they were very proud of the way we were conducting business.

By 10 a.m., sales had really picked up, and Mommy and Mrs. Santos, Zoë's mom pitched in to help while we were each busy with customers of our own.

By 2:45 p.m., the baked goods were almost gone, and the driveway was now only half-full. The cash box was stuffed with $1's, $5's, $10's and $20's, and people were still showing up. Wow, my signs advertising the sale really worked!

By 5 p.m., the number of customers had decreased, the inventory was low, and we were pooped, so we decided to take down the balloons and stop for the day. Mommy fixed us dinner while Daddy and Mr. Kyoko packed the few unsold items onto Daddy's pick-up truck to donate to a local charity.

The Evaluation

After dinner, we sat on the floor in front of the television in the family room and began to count the money. "$50...$100...$200...$300...." I kept counting as everyone watched, amazed by how well we had done. "$400...$500...$600..."

"We made a total profit of $728!" I hollered. Then, we all began to shout and dance around the room.

"Wow, we're rich!" Chef exclaimed. We divided the profit by four, and each received $182.

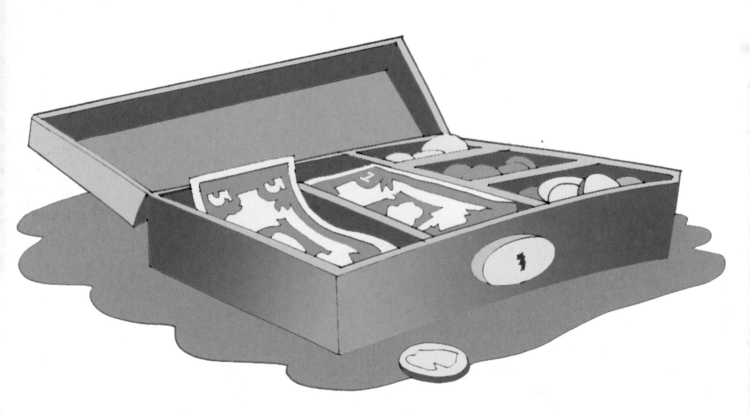

On Monday, PopPop, our grandfather drove Chef and me to the bank where Mrs. Anderson, the bank manager helped us open individual savings accounts.

She explained the program to us, gave us our official savings deposit book and a certificate to hang up at home.

We had a lot of fun and we each received an additional $25 just for opening a new account!

The following Saturday, I finally got my bike. It felt great when I handed my own money over to the man behind the counter, waited for my receipt and rode out of the store with my new bike. I did it!

Then, Mommy and Daddy took Chef and me to Druid Hill Park and we all rode our bikes around the lake in the warm sunshine.

As I was getting ready for bed that night, Mommy said, "Your father and I are very proud of the way you planned and worked for your bike."

"We're even prouder of the way you and Chef decided to save a portion of your money in a bank account," Daddy added. "That's very smart."

Then they kissed me good night and turned off the light. I closed my eyes and was soon dreaming of the great day I had riding my bike at the park by the lake, chasing the birds as they flew away.

Lessons Learned

New Vocabulary: Business Terms

advertising: calling something to the attention of the public, especially by paid announcements

bank: a place of business that lends, exchanges, takes care of, or issues money

business plan: a method or sketch of arranging something for the purpose of achieving a business goal

customer: a person that buys a product or service

donate: to make a gift of; to give away

inventory: the stock of goods on hand

marketing: to offer for sale in a marketplace

profit: the remaining money after all the expenses are subtracted from the total amount received

savings account: an account on which interest is usually paid and from which withdrawals can be made

sell: to achieve a sale

Team Project

Break children into teams and guide them as they put together a basic business plan to raise money for school supplies, a class party, a community function or a charity event, etc. (This can be a class project at school or a family project at home.) Starting a business is a great way for kids to learn life skills and build self-confidence. They should consider the following guidelines:

A)   Set Realistic Goals

B)   Conduct Proper Preparation (cost, time, research, desired outcome, etc.)

C)   Be Safe

D)   Plan Marketing Strategy

E)   Determine How They Will Measure Success/Evaluation

F)   Most of All, It Should Be Fun!

Chef's Favorite "Sweet-Potato Cookies"

Sweet potato, an ingredient frequently used in African cuisine, adds flavor and a bright orange color to this cake-like snack.

COOKIE DOUGH

10 tablespoons margarine or butter

1/4 cup sugar

1 tablespoon lemon zest

2 teaspoons freshly ground nutmeg

1/4 cup honey

1 egg

1 cup finely grated raw sweet potato

2 1/2 cups all-purpose flour

1 1/2 teaspoons baking powder

1/2 teaspoon baking soda

1/2 teaspoon salt

LEMON GLAZE

2 teaspoons butter

1–2 tablespoons lemon juice

1 1/2 cups powdered sugar

1 tablespoon water

1. Cream together the margarine or butter and sugar in a large bowl. Blend in the lemon zest, nutmeg, honey and egg. Fold in the sweet potato.

2. In a separate bowl, sift the flour, baking powder, baking soda and salt. Then, slowly add it to the first mixture and stir until well blended.

3. Arrange the cookie dough by rounded teaspoonfuls on ungreased cookie sheets. Bake at 350 degrees for 7-9 minutes. Makes about 60 cookies.

4. To make the lemon glaze, combine all ingredients in a separate bowl until smooth. A more water by the drop until glaze is easy to spread on the cooled cookies.

Inspired by Valerie Nelson
I want to thank my mother for creating Hillary and inspiring me to give her life.
I want to thank both of my parents for always supporting my inner Hillary. I love you.
- L.N.

To my wonderful family-- my wife Autier and my sons, Jaylen and Aren. Thank you for your support.
Love
Jerry aka Dad

Nelson Publishing, LLC
Entertain. Educate. Empower.
12138 Central Avenue, Suite 477, Mitchellville, Maryland 20721
www.nelson-publishing.com

Hillary's BIG Business Adventure/ by Lori Nelson; Illustrations by Jerry Craft.
Summary: Highlights a young girl's ability to create a business opportunity that enables her to earn the funds she needs to purchase a new bicycle.

ISBN-10: 0-9794171-0-4
ISBN-13: 978-0-9794171-0-8

To The Parents: Children can learn valuable skills by starting a business, and those who learn to save at an early age ⁀e an even greater advantage. CNN reported that some financial experts believe our spending and saving habits are ⁀d as young as 5 years old, deciding whether we'll end up as spenders or savers. Good habits should start early in ⁀ developing your child's money management skills is critical to their future. Start now, and lead by example!